::::orca
limelights

Warm Up

Sara Leach

ORCA BOOK PUBLISHERS

Library and Archives Canada Cataloguing in Publication

Leach, Sara, 1971-, author
Warm up / Sara Leach.
(Orca limelights)

Issued in print and electronic formats.
ISBN 978-1-4598-0428-9 (pbk.).--ISBN 978-1-4598-0429-6 (pdf).--
ISBN 978-1-4598-0430-2 (epub)

I. Title. II. Series: Orca limelights
PS8623.E253W37 2014   jc813'.6   C2013-906638-1
                                               C2013-906639-x

First published in the United States, 2014
Library of Congress Control Number: 2013951382

Summary: Jasmine's dance team is falling apart, just before a competition,
and it's up to Jasmine to figure out a way to bring the team together.

MIX
Paper from
responsible sources
FSC® C004071

ANCIENT FOREST ™
FRIENDLY

*Orca Book Publishers is dedicated to preserving the environment and has
printed this book on Forest Stewardship Council® certified paper.*

Orca Book Publishers gratefully acknowledges the support for
its publishing programs provided by the following agencies:
the Government of Canada through the Canada Book Fund and the
Canada Council for the Arts, and the Province of British Columbia
through the BC Arts Council and the Book Publishing Tax Credit.

Design by Teresa Bubela
Cover photography by Getty Images

ORCA BOOK PUBLISHERS
PO Box 5626, STN. B
Victoria, BC Canada
V8R 6S4

ORCA BOOK PUBLISHERS
PO Box 468
Custer, WA USA
98240-0468

www.orcabook.com
Printed and bound in Canada.

17 16 15 14 • 4 3 2 1

For Michelle,
who looked fabulous in a sequined tube top.

One

Jasmine unfolded her leg into a high kick, remembering to keep her shoulders down and her toes pointed. Miss Carina gestured from offstage, drawing exaggerated lines beside her mouth. Jasmine frowned for a moment, trying to figure out what her teacher meant.

Oh. Smile. Jasmine pasted a smile on her face as she and the other seven members of her dance team ran into a V formation in front of the competition judges. They began their pirouettes. Jasmine was off tempo and finished slightly behind the rest of her teammates. She rushed her chassé to catch up for the finale.

Miss Carina's voice played in her head. *And one and two and reach.*

Jasmine caught herself frowning again and then smiled for the judges, hoping she had only been counting in her head. She could see her mom and Grandma Verbenka in the audience, but she quickly looked away so they wouldn't distract her.

She split-leaped past Felicity, who looked anxious. Jasmine smiled even harder, trying to remind her teammate to wipe the worry off her face.

They were almost done. Only a few more steps. Only a few more chances to wow the judges. She landed her last split leap as the music paused for a beat and then began its final phrase. As the piano notes began to build and the singer's soulful voice belted out the lyrics, Jasmine stepped back, knowing that the rest of the team was doing the same. Half turn. Step forward with her left foot. The girls faced each other in a circle. The music rose to a crescendo. Each girl raised her right arm, reached across the circle and joined hands with a partner.

Jasmine clasped Melanie's forearm as they had done so many times in practice. Gripping hard, they fell away from each other into a layback, looking out at the audience with their backs arched and their heads facing the floor.

She loved the idea of this move. To the audience they would look like a sunflower, their heads like petals emerging from the center. The reality was that it hurt, and more than once someone had fallen.

Hold, two, three. Jasmine felt her grip loosen on Melanie. *Please hold on*, she told herself. *Don't fall today.*

She squeezed as hard as she could and raised her body back up. With a grin at Melanie, she rose on her toes, then dropped to the floor and slid outward on her side. As one, she and the rest of the team rolled onto their stomachs, pushed themselves to their feet and ran to their final formation. Jasmine sank to one knee in front of Felicity, with Chelsea and Shira beside her and the other four girls fanned out behind them. They scooped their left arms out and up and dropped them in unison with the final chord. The music ended. Jasmine smiled, trying not to show how hard she was breathing as the audience applauded.

They'd done it. No falls. No major errors.

"Ready, and…" Chelsea called over the applause.

They all stood, formed a line and filed off the stage.

Miss Carina nodded as they walked past her. "Good job. We'll talk in the dressing room."

Jasmine followed her teammates through the large warm-up hall behind the ballroom that held the stage. She could see the girls from InMotion, the last group to perform, finishing the preparations for their number.

"Don't even look at them," whispered Shira.

"I can't help it," Jasmine said. "They always look so sharp, even when they're lining up to go onstage. Their hair is perfect, their costumes are perfect. They even stand exactly the same way."

"We look sharp too," Shira said. "Maybe one of them will fall."

"Shira!" Jasmine gasped. "You shouldn't wish bad luck on another team."

"Why not?" Shira asked. "I'm sure they were wishing it on us."

Shira was probably right, Jasmine thought. The InMotion team had never shown any signs of kindness toward her team, Moondance. She and her teammates had to walk right past InMotion to reach their assigned dressing room.

One of the girls from InMotion snickered at Jasmine. "Can't keep your eyes off the best, can you?"

Jasmine looked away. She couldn't think of anything to say.

"Break a leg," Shira said in a sickly sweet voice.

Somehow Jasmine didn't think she meant it as good luck.

Miss Carina shooed them into the dressing room. Two other teams were putting on warm-up suits after their dances. The Moondance girls moved as far away from the other teams as possible, so that they could talk freely.

"I messed up twice," Felicity moaned, grabbing her hoodie from the zippered garment bag with her name on it.

"When?" Melanie asked. "I didn't see anything." She checked her hair in the mirror, smoothing back the small wisps.

"On my chaînés, and I got stuck sliding into the final move."

Jasmine peeked over Melanie's shoulder into the mirror. Her straight brown hair was still shellacked into place. It was one advantage to having hair that never curled no matter how hard she worked with a curling iron.

"Girls," Miss Carina called. The chatter stopped, and all eyes turned to look at her. "Don't pick apart what you did. There were some mistakes. But the dance is over. All we can hope for is that the other teams don't do any better."

Jasmine raised her eyebrows at Shira. Was that supposed to be a pep talk? It wasn't exactly over the top with congratulations. Shouldn't they be focused on their own performance, not on what the other teams did?

Shira shrugged and mouthed, "InMotion."

Jasmine nodded.

"Can we go watch the last number?" Melanie asked.

"If you hurry," Miss Carina said. "They'll be starting any moment. But go in quietly. The judges will dock points from our team if you cause a disturbance. Put something warm over your costumes, but leave them on underneath."

They were all hoping for an award, and they would need to be in costume to receive it. The Moondance studio hadn't ever placed in the Star Struck finals competition, and InMotion, run by Miss Brandi, Miss Carina's biggest rival, had placed first for the last six years. Rumor had it that Miss Carina and Miss Brandi had danced together when they were younger, but after Miss Brandi left to join the Royal Winnipeg Ballet, she'd never treated Miss Carina the same. Miss Carina had opened Moondance, and a few years later, Miss Brandi had retired from performing and opened her own studio. Miss Carina had been desperate to prove that her studio was as good as InMotion ever since.

The most important thing today was to make it to the finals in June. To do that, they had to get at least third place. But if they could take first place in this preliminary competition, it would send a message to InMotion that Moondance was a force to be reckoned with.

Shira held open the door to the large ball-room and put her finger to her lips. The team crept in without a word and found a row of empty seats at the back. Jasmine spotted her mom. She wanted to wave or call out to get her attention, but her mom and grandmother had their eyes on the stage.

The InMotion team filed onto the stage, and a cheer went up from the crowd. It was a big team—twenty dancers, which meant they had a lot of fans rooting for them in the audience. That gave them an advantage over Moondance, the smallest team in their category. Cheering and clapping always made dancing easier, whether you were on a real stage in a real theater or in a big hotel conference room like this one.

The first beats of the music started, and Jasmine's eyes focused on the stage again. Her heart sank. The InMotion girls might not be nice, but they were great dancers. Every move they made was precise and on time. On their triple pirouettes, their heads all snapped to the front at the same moment. Their split leaps were high, their legs straight, their toes pointed. But more than that, they had confidence. You could feel it radiating from the stage. They didn't just smile. It was almost like they were talking with the audience. They communicated their joy of dance through their whole bodies.

Their cheering section went wild as they hit their final pose and then strode off the stage.

"We're hooped," Felicity said, clapping halfheartedly.

"Yup," said Melanie. "We don't stand a chance."

"Let's hope for third place at least. That's all that really matters," Chelsea said.

InMotion's dance had been the last number of the competition. Now they all had to wait for the judges to tally the scores and announce the awards. Jasmine fidgeted in her seat. Clearly, InMotion was better than their team. But what about the other groups? She hadn't been able to watch them, because Moondance had been getting ready to perform. Would Moondance be good enough?

She looked down the line of seats at her team. Everyone was sitting forward in anticipation. From a distance, they all looked the same—a row of buns, identical makeup and navy hoodies. But on closer inspection, differences became obvious. Shira's curly brown hair never stayed long in its bun, no matter how much hair spray she used. She pulled at one of the fluffy curls as she waited. Chelsea's dark skin contrasted sharply with Felicity's pale skin and freckles. Andrea's big chest and hips were surprising on a dancer, but she was still very good. Darveet and Robyn were gripping each other's arms, Robyn a full head shorter than Darveet. Melanie, her blond hair in a perfect bun, was almost falling off her seat, she was sitting so far forward.

Jasmine stretched her legs under the seat in front of her. She was one of the tallest girls on the team, even though she was the youngest. Her grandmother always said she had a dancer's body. Jasmine was just glad she'd inherited a slender frame and didn't look like a sturdy Russian peasant the way so many of her relatives did.

After what felt like an hour but was probably only five minutes, the head judge climbed onto the stage, holding a microphone. "Thank you to our competitors. You've all done a fantastic job. Our top three teams will advance to the finals of the Star Struck competition in one month's time." The crowd cheered.

Jasmine's stomach turned over. *Please let us make it to the finals.* Everyone on her team wanted it so badly. They wanted to prove they had what it took to be great dancers. And besides, Miss Carina would flip if they didn't.

The judge pulled out some sheets of paper. "In third place, Moondance Studio."

Jasmine leaped to her feet and hugged her teammates.

"We made it!" Shira cried. They unzipped their hoodies, threw them onto their seats and ran to the stage to receive their ribbons.

"In second place," the judge said, "Dance for Life!" One of the groups that Jasmine had seen in the dressing room ran squealing up to the stage, the sequins on their green costumes glimmering in the lights.

"And now, the moment you've been waiting for. In first place—and a full ten points ahead of anyone else in the competition—InMotion!" As he shouted the words, the InMotion team and its entourage went crazy. Jasmine winced at the noise.

The InMotion girls, in their red-and-black leotards, ran up to the stage, jumping and hugging. Jasmine had to force herself to keep smiling. She was glad Moondance had made it to the finals, but first place would have been better.

Two

Jasmine climbed the stairs to the studio, her hair slicked into a tight bun, wearing her practice leotard and tights full of holes. The stairwell smelled of sweat, stinky shoes and hair spray. For the hundredth time, her eyes scanned the notices and studio rules posted on the wall.

Arrive early. Be prepared to start on time.

Respect your instructor, respect the studio, respect your classmates.

Vancouver Modern Dance Festival, June 12-24, 2013.

Why hadn't anyone bothered to take that one down? The event had happened ages ago.

"Hey, Jaz," Shira said as Jasmine opened the studio door. "Miss Carina wants to meet with the team before warm-up."

Jasmine nodded, pulled her water bottle out of her bag and went to sit by the mirrors with the rest of the team. She was two minutes early, but everyone else was already there, sitting in their colorful leotards. They all knew how strict Miss Carina was about being on time. Nobody wanted to do extra stomach crunches—the consequence of being late to practice. Jasmine knew that she was cutting it close, but her mom had driven her, and she didn't get off work in time to drop Jasmine any earlier.

The girls were whispering quietly among themselves. Jasmine leaned over to Chelsea, the oldest member of the team, the best dancer and the unofficial leader. "What's the meeting about?"

Chelsea shrugged. "No idea."

Miss Carina came out of her office a few seconds later. She was holding a small trophy and a sheet of paper. As usual, she wore a baby-pink ballet sweater, a black leotard and a short black wraparound skirt over pink tights. She stood with a frown on her face, her gray hair pulled into such a tight bun that her eyebrows had to struggle to form a V. Her ribs and collarbones were visible under the pale veined skin of her chest. Her right foot, turned out in fourth position, tapped impatiently while she waited for the girls to settle onto the floor in front of her.

"Well, girls," she said. "We've made it to the finals." She didn't look too happy about it. "The competition will be difficult. And InMotion danced better than you."

Jasmine hugged her knees to her chest and rested her chin on them. So much for being happy with third place. It was all about beating InMotion, even for Miss Carina. Especially for Miss Carina.

"The judges liked the extension of your legs, and they made a special note about the layback. But they thought you could be challenged with more difficult moves. And they also felt that there wasn't enough emotion in the piece."

Jasmine agreed with the judges about the emotion. After seeing InMotion perform again, she understood. Not that she knew how to do what they'd done. But she wasn't sure about adding more difficult moves.

"It's a lyrical piece," Shira said. "It's not supposed to be full of fancy moves."

Miss Carina glared at Shira. "Don't interrupt!" She paused. "A lyrical number can be challenging. It doesn't have a lot of jumps, lifts and acro, but it can still be difficult."

Miss Carina cleared her throat and put the trophy on the floor. "I want you girls to have the best chance possible at the finals. Therefore, we're going to focus on the judges' recommendations. I'm going to rework the dance, starting today."

Jasmine covered her mouth to suppress a groan. She could barely keep up as it was. Everyone else on the team had been competing for at least one full year before this one. Jasmine was the only newcomer. She could barely remember the choreography they'd already learned and had to work on her turns and kicks every day to make sure she could do them onstage. How could she perform an even harder dance?

"But we'll never be tight enough for the finals if we learn something new now," Melanie said.

Miss Carina straightened, her eyes glinting. "Nonsense. We have a month. I've seen you girls learn the ending to a dance the night before a performance, and nobody could tell the difference."

She nodded once to signal the end of the meeting. "Let's warm up."

The girls spread out across the floor. The music started and Miss Carina led them through the first few steps of the warm-up. Jasmine pliéd, bending her knees in a wide second position, sweeping her arms out and then up to meet above her head, breathing deeply as Adele's voice rang through the studio. This was one of her favorite moves. Something about the air filling her lungs, and the first stretches of her body, always made her feel joyful. She loved the song too. Sometimes she wished they danced to this song onstage. Adele's music would be perfect for lyrical. She didn't mind their song—it was by some singer she had never heard of—but it didn't inspire her the way the warm-up music did.

As the warm-up continued, however, Jasmine's joy turned to pain and sweat. Miss Carina seemed determined to push them to their limits through all parts of the class, not just choreography. They did so many tendus—sliding their feet across the floor, then pointing their toes while holding their arms out straight at shoulder height—that Jasmine thought her arms might fall off.

"No dropping your arms," Miss Carina said. "If they're tired, engage your back muscles. The stronger you are, the better you'll be able to dance."

Jasmine knew this was true, but it still hurt. No sooner had they finished their tendus and kicks than they were on the floor for stomach crunches and push-ups. Jasmine had always thought it strange that the whole first part of class was called warm-up. In most sports, warm-up lasted fifteen minutes and was all about getting ready to do the sport. In dance, warm-up lasted most of the class and included strength, stretching and technique training.

They began their floor stretches. This was another part of warm-up that Jasmine loved. Stretching came more easily to her than the strength moves. But today, even the stretching was difficult.

Jasmine spread her legs in a straddle and reached forward along the floor. Miss Carina came over and pressed against her back. "Keep your toes pointed and your knees facing the ceiling." As soon as Jasmine turned her knees up, her leg muscles started to protest, and she had to back off the stretch.

"Rolling your knees forward is cheating," Miss Carina said. "It allows you to stretch farther, but it's a bad habit. Knees to the ceiling, always."

Miss Carina circled around the class, barking out instructions and giving pieces of advice. By the time warm-up was finished, Jasmine's legs felt like cooked spaghetti. And they still had to do their choreography.

She stumbled to the side of the room, gulped down some water and began pulling on her foot thongs, small pieces of leather that protected the bottom of her feet and allowed her to turn and slide more easily.

Miss Carina clapped her hands. "Move it, girls. Get into your starting positions."

Jasmine sipped more water and staggered to her place at the back left of the group. She moved into the window of space between Chelsea and Darveet, checking that she could see herself in the mirror. She wanted to be sure the audience could see her if she was onstage.

All eight girls were sweaty and red-cheeked. At least Jasmine wasn't the only one hurting from warm-up. The temperature in the studio had climbed steadily as their body heat rose.

Jasmine didn't bother asking if she could open a window. She knew Miss Carina would tell her how dangerous cold air could be for a dancer's muscles. But what about the damage the stuffy air was doing to their lungs? Jasmine had always wanted to ask but had never had the guts.

"For now we'll stick with our formations," Miss Carina said. "I may change them later, depending on how everyone is dancing."

Jasmine felt a ripple of excitement go through the team, especially the back row. Everyone wanted to be in front. Jasmine knew from watching other groups perform that the audience mostly watched the front row. You had to make a concerted effort to watch the girls in the back. It was parents watching their kids who noticed the ones in behind. Miss Carina never said it outright, but she always managed to put the best dancers in front. It made sense, but it didn't seem fair.

"We'll start with the same opening, but instead of double chaînés, I want triples."

"In the same amount of time?" Chelsea asked.

"Of course in the same amount of time," Miss Carina barked. "You'll have to move your feet faster. And don't forget to spot."

Everyone nodded. Chaînés were two half turns linked together. You stepped out facing the mirror with your right foot, then stepped with your left to face the back wall. Usually they did that twice in a row—double chaînés. Now they'd have to do it three times. Not too big a deal—in warm-up, they often did a whole row of them across the floor—but they'd have to be quick to fit three to the music.

Spotting was looking at one spot in the direction you were going for as long as possible, and then whipping your head around at the last second. It stopped dancers from getting dizzy and throwing up when they did a lot of turns.

"From the top," Miss Carina said.

Jasmine knelt down in her opening position, with her head on her knees. The first slow bars of the music started, and she counted along in her head. Four counts of gentle guitar and piano during which nobody moved. On count five, the girls in the front row began pulsing to the music. On seven, Jasmine and her row joined in. Together, they lifted halfway up, not looking at the audience, then folded back down over their knees. Sweeping one arm out to the side and up to the ceiling, then the other, they bobbed and floated over their knees like butterflies, then swept both arms up and rose to their feet, looking at the mirror for the first time.

They floated their arms to their sides, paused and started their chaînés as the lyrics began. Jasmine kept her feet close together and her arms in tight, trying to turn as fast as she could. She felt the room spinning around her even after she stopped, and it took her a moment to realize she hadn't quite finished her final turn and was out of place in the dance.

"Cut!" yelled Miss Carina. She paused the music. "Girls, I told you to spot. Those chaînés were terrible. Try it again without the music."

Everyone went back to their opening positions, and Miss Carina counted out the music. "And one and two and three and first group up and six and second group and one all together. Arms up. And chaînés. Spot! Spot! Spot!"

This time, Jasmine remembered to spot. She completed her third turn and was facing the right direction in the right place.

"Again!" cried Miss Carina. "Better spotting, but Jasmine and Felicity, you're too slow."

Back they went. On the third try, Jasmine got it right, but Melanie was off. Finally, on the fifth run-through, Miss Carina deemed it correct, and they were able to try again with the music. Fifteen minutes of working on choreography, and they'd only made it through three counts of eight. They still had two full minutes of the dance to work on. How would they ever be ready in time for finals?

Three

At practice two days later, Jasmine opened the door into the studio stairwell to find Shira pulling off her shoes.

"Man," her friend said. "I'm so stiff I can hardly bend over."

"Me too!" Jasmine said, glad to hear that someone else was sore after their Tuesday practice. "Do you think she's going to make us work that hard again today?"

"Probably harder. Maybe she'll make us do pirouettes for an hour and a half today, instead of chaînés."

Jasmine giggled. "Maybe we'll get to move on to the tenth second of the song."

"Let's hope so."

Melanie popped her head out of the door to the studio. "Shira and Jasmine. Hurry up!"

Shira looked at Melanie, then at Jasmine, and raised her eyebrows. "Who made her the dance police?"

Jasmine shrugged and started up the stairs.

They went into the studio, put their water bottles away and joined the team, which was already in position for warm-up. Jasmine noticed that, like her, everyone was wearing as little as possible today. Even though the weather was cool for May, she had on her spaghetti-strap leotard and her dance shorts instead of tights. The rest of the team was similarly dressed. Everyone knew it would be hot in the studio today.

Usually the dancers stood in pretty much the same spots each week, with Jasmine, Shira, Felicity and Melanie in the back, and the more experienced dancers—Chelsea, Robyn, Darveet and Andrea—in the front. But it was different today. Melanie had staked out a spot front and center, forcing Robyn to move to the back.

Shira and Jasmine looked at each other, and Shira raised her eyebrows again. What was going on?

Miss Carina walked in, nodded to the girls and started the music. As Jasmine lifted her arms in the opening plié sequence, her muscles groaned in protest. It was still her favorite move of the warm-up, and if this move hurt, she was in trouble.

Melanie seemed to be glowing and was taking up as much space in front of the mirror as she could. Every time Jasmine moved to get a better view of Miss Carina, Melanie would move too, blocking her. After they'd done their kicks, tendus and pliés and were doing their standing straddle stretch, Melanie looked through her legs and called back, "Jasmine, straighten your knees."

Jasmine grimaced as she looked at her knees, which did have an ever-so-slight bend in them. What made Melanie suddenly decide that she was the teacher?

Nobody else noticed except for Shira, who turned her head toward Jasmine, screwed up her face and stuck out her tongue. She looked so funny doing it upside down that Jasmine broke into giggles.

"Jasmine," shouted Miss Carina. "Focus on your stretching!"

Jasmine turned her head back to the floor. That wasn't fair. Why hadn't Miss Carina said anything to Melanie? Had she ignored Melanie on purpose?

By the end of the warm-up, Jasmine felt like a pile of wet rags. She was also ready to slap Melanie, who'd called instructions to her two more times without getting caught. The only good news was that Melanie would have to move to her place in the back row for choreography.

Jasmine pulled on her foot thongs, drank some water and hurried to her opening spot for the dance.

"Girls, I'm going to make a placement change for the opening formation of our dance," Miss Carina said. "Melanie and Chelsea, switch positions, please. You are about the same height, so nobody else needs to switch."

A silence fell over the girls as Melanie strode to Chelsea's spot.

Shira wiggled her eyebrows. Jasmine knew exactly what she was thinking. Melanie had known the switch was coming. That's why she'd been acting like such a diva during warm-up.

Chelsea obviously hadn't known about the switch. Her mouth had dropped open at the announcement. Then she'd snapped it shut. Jasmine was sure she heard her teeth clash together. As Chelsea walked into the back row, her cheeks flamed red.

Jasmine felt a bit sorry for Chelsea, but it wasn't like she was being kicked off the team or anything. There were only two rows. She wasn't being banished to Siberia. Jasmine tried to smile at her, but Chelsea wouldn't meet her eyes.

Miss Carina clapped to get their attention. "I'd like to finish the first section of the dance today. Run through the bars we worked on last class."

The girls knelt down for the opening, and Miss Carina counted them in. "Five, six, seven, eight."

They ran through the opening, including the new triple chaînés, then stopped and looked at their teacher. Jasmine could tell everyone was holding their breath, waiting for her critique.

She nodded. "Not bad. Your chaînés are looking better, but you still need to hold your spots longer. We're going to move forward."

Jasmine let her breath out. *Finally.*

"The next section is our partner work. Chelsea, your new partner is Jasmine. Melanie, you're partnered with Darveet. Walk through the moves."

The girls returned to the spots where they had finished their chaînés. Miss Carina counted them in again, and they pushed back, swiveled and jazz-walked over to their partners, in a staggered line of four pairs.

It felt strange to work with Chelsea instead of Melanie. Jasmine had never done any partner work with her before. They reached their hands out and pressed them together in front of their chests, then drew back, turning away and looking at the floor before rejoining hands and then resting their heads on each other's shoulders.

"Stop there," Miss Carina said. "I want you to run it from the top to here. I'm not making any changes to this section."

Jasmine breathed a sigh of relief and smiled at Chelsea, but Chelsea didn't smile back. She turned away and went to her spot.

They ran the piece again. When they got to the end of the section, Miss Carina stopped the music and let out a grunt of frustration. "Girls, you're missing the point of this number."

Jasmine frowned. What on earth was Miss Carina talking about?

"This is lyrical, not jazz. The reason it's called lyrical is because it's like poetry—it expresses emotion. I want you to feel that emotion. What's this story about?" She looked at the team. Melanie raised her hand. "Yes, Melanie?"

"It's about a girl who has to leave her family to go on a journey. When she gets where she's going, she has no friends. But then she makes friends and celebrates."

Miss Carina flashed a rare smile at Melanie. "Exactly! I'm glad you've been paying attention."

Chelsea rolled her eyes. Jasmine was surprised—usually Chelsea was so supportive of everyone on the team.

Miss Carina's eyes roamed over the girls. "I want to feel that you're sad to be leaving your family. Even when we're practicing, I want to see it."

Jasmine had no idea how to do what Miss Carina wanted. She looked at her teammates. Most of them were nodding, as though what their teacher had said made perfect sense. There was no way she was going to ask Miss Carina to explain though. Not after the way she'd been biting everyone's heads off lately.

"Right, try it again."

They ran the piece again. Jasmine tried to show emotion. Instead of smiling, she frowned—when she remembered to. But most of the time, she was busy thinking about the steps. Wasn't it better to get the moves right and not fall or run into anyone?

Miss Carina clapped her hands, signaling them to stop and listen. "A little better, most of you. But Jasmine, I can almost see you counting. This is lyrical. Show me the feeling."

Jasmine felt her face flush. She hated being singled out. Shira made a detour on her way back to her spot and gave Jasmine a squeeze on the arm.

They started again. Miss Carina called out over the music, "You're waking up, happy to see the new day. Come on, girls, let's see some joy on those faces!"

Jasmine spread her arms in the opening moves, stretching her lips into a smile.

"Now you're meeting with your family. You learn that you have to leave. You don't want to, which is why you push away, but you know you must go."

Jasmine laid her head on Chelsea's shoulder. What move came next? Right, the formation change.

"Keep going," Miss Carina said.

The girls pushed away from each other and ran into a long line circling the room and forming a semicircle facing the mirror.

"Stop there, girls. Run it again."

By the end of practice, they had made it through another three bars of music. Jasmine slumped against the wall and took off her foot thongs. "This is going to take forever," she said to Chelsea.

Chelsea shrugged. "We want to be good for the finals." She stepped into the alcove where she'd left her water bottle, pushing past Melanie.

"Hey!" Melanie said. "Watch out."

"Stop taking up so much room, then," Chelsea said. She scooped up her clothes. "C'mon, Darveet, my mom'll be waiting." As she and Darveet moved into the stairwell, Chelsea leaned in and whispered something to her. Darveet nodded and giggled, and then they ran down the stairs and out of sight.

Four

At the next class, Chelsea pushed open the door as Melanie and Jasmine were taking off their rain boots. "Hi, Jasmine," she said.

"Hey, Chelsea."

Chelsea pulled off her boots and stomped up the stairs without even looking at Melanie.

"Hey!" Melanie said. "Aren't you going to say hi to me?"

Chelsea stopped and let out a long sigh, her back to Melanie, then quickly looked over her shoulder and said a quick "Hi."

Melanie's face turned red. She stormed up the stairs after Chelsea, grabbed her arm and spun her around. "I didn't ask to trade spots, you know. Miss Carina was the one who decided to do it."

"Well, you didn't have to be such a big show-off and mirror hog about it!" Chelsea yelled.

"Maybe it's time someone else got the front! You've always been Little Miss Perfect, but there are other people in the class who can dance too!"

"I know that! But at least when I'm in the front, I don't block everybody else."

Melanie's face turned even redder. "You're jealous because you aren't the best dancer in the class anymore." She turned and ran up the rest of the stairs, yanking open the door to the studio, running through and slamming it behind her.

Chelsea stood in the stairwell for another minute. Jasmine watched from the bottom of the stairs. She had a feeling Chelsea had forgotten she was there, and she held her breath, trying not to make any sound. Finally, Chelsea tipped her chin up, rolled her shoulders a few times and marched up the rest of the stairs.

Jasmine waited for another minute before following her. This was going to be an interesting class.

It turned out to be a long, painful class full of snide looks and bickering. Melanie and Chelsea jockeyed for a spot in front of the mirror the entire time. Whenever there was a break, Chelsea ran over to Darveet and started whispering. Melanie and Felicity spent their breaks in the opposite corner with their heads bent together.

Jasmine tried to ignore them all. As soon as class ended, she grabbed her stuff and bolted for the door.

* * *

At school on Friday, Jasmine dropped into a seat at the lunch table next to her friend Will. She groaned as she bent her sore legs to sit.

"Another hard class?" Will asked.

Jasmine nodded. "Killer."

Will was also a Moondance student, but he wasn't on the dance team. He took hip-hop and funk classes from another teacher.

"Miss Carina still on a tear?" he asked.

"Oh yeah. Yesterday we worked for half an hour on eight counts of music. It was so painful. She made us do it, like, fifty times, and then, after all that, she changed it! I was so mad."

Will shook his head. "Why'd she change it?"

"Because she said we weren't doing it right. Maybe she wasn't teaching it right."

Will laughed. "Did you say that to her?"

"Yeah, right. Can you imagine?"

Will stood up, blocking the aisle between the lunch tables. He imitated Jasmine. "Miss Carina, we aren't the problem, you are!" Then he turned around to face the other way. He sucked in his cheeks, stood like he had a pole up his back and turned his feet out.

Jasmine started to laugh. He was standing exactly like her teacher.

"Jasmine Natasha Verbenka!" he screeched. Kids at tables all around them were staring, but Will didn't pay any attention. "Get out in the hallway and give me five hundred stomach crunches. Then you come back in here and kiss my feet until you've learned some respect!"

Jasmine laughed so hard that orange juice sprayed out of her mouth and landed on his shoes.

"That will be another thousand crunches!"

As Will sat down, Jasmine tried to mop the orange juice off his shoes with a napkin.

"Don't worry—they looked too new anyway."

A shadow appeared over them. "You shouldn't be making fun of Miss Carina like that. She's a good teacher."

Jasmine looked up. It was Melanie, the only other member of the Moondance team who went to her school.

"Uh, right, Melanie. Because you've never complained about her before," Will said.

Melanie stood with her arms crossed over her chest, her feet turned out and one leg in fourth position in front of her. She looked exactly like the dancers in a famous Degas painting. Or like Miss Carina. Jasmine wondered if she'd practiced standing like that.

"She makes us work hard, but she gets results."

"We're just having fun, Melanie. Lighten up," Jasmine said.

Melanie sniffed.

"It's not like I was imitating you," Will said. "But I could."

Jasmine snorted more orange juice. Melanie stalked off, swishing her blond hair behind her. "No thanks," she said over her shoulder. "See you later."

"What was that all about?" Will asked. "She used to be nice. And I've heard her complain about Miss Carina hundreds of times."

"I told you, being moved to the front spot has gone right to her head. It's like Miss Carina told her that she was the star of the team or something."

"Maybe she did."

Jasmine thought about that. Melanie had known ahead of time that she would be moved, which meant she and Miss Carina had had a one-on-one at some point. Who knew what Miss Carina had said? Maybe Will was right.

They watched Melanie glide through the lunchroom. Her head barely moved up and down as she walked. She'd definitely been practicing walking like a dancer.

Jasmine turned to Will. "If Miss Carina meant to make things better by singling out Melanie, she made a big mistake. She's created a monster, and our team is falling apart. Chelsea and Melanie aren't speaking to each other. Darveet has joined up with Chelsea. Felicity is siding with Melanie, and Andrea, Shira, Robyn and I are stuck in the middle."

"Sounds like a party," Will said.

"It's the worst. Too bad you aren't on the team. It would be way more fun."

"No way," Will said.

"Why not? You're good enough."

"I don't want to be the only boy on a team of girls." He grinned. "Everybody would start fighting over me, and then you'd be in even worse trouble than before."

Jasmine rolled her eyes and swatted him on the arm. "You wish!" But he was probably right. Will was very good-looking, with sandy blond hair, bright green eyes and a wide, mischievous smile. She knew that many of her girlfriends had crushes on him. He might cause some problems if he were on the team. To her though, he'd always just be Will, her friend since grade three.

"Besides," he said, "I only like hip-hop."

"You haven't tried anything else!" Jasmine said.

"Not true. When I first started dancing, my mom put me in tap, ballet and jazz." He scrunched up his nose and stuck out his tongue. "She keeps a picture of me in a frog costume on her dresser. Don't make me relive that experience."

Jasmine opened her mouth to protest, but the bell rang.

"Time to go," Will said, standing up and shoving his water bottle into his backpack. "Another scintillating afternoon of learning awaits us."

"Uh-huh," Jasmine said. "Math and social studies. Yahoo. I'd almost rather be doing stomach crunches."

Five

At practice on Tuesday, Jasmine's arms felt slightly less tired when they did their tendus and push-ups. Maybe Miss Carina had been right. Dancing was easier when you were stronger. She was still hot, sweaty and tired by the end of warm-up though.

Miss Carina began teaching them the next section of the dance, which was almost completely changed from the old version. "This part of the dance is the journey. The music turns dark and forceful. Listen for the cellos that are highlighted in this section. You're angry at having to leave, and you take it out on the creatures you meet along the way. Watch." She strode and turned across the room, making complicated moves with her arms and feet. She looked so angry that Jasmine took a step away. Miss Carina stopped and turned off the music. "You'll be in partners. One person will be the girl, the other a creature of the forest."

Jasmine was glad they already had costumes. What if Miss Carina had made half of them wear antlers or fake fur?

"Shira, Jasmine, Darveet and Chelsea, you will be the girls in this section. The rest of you, go sit down and stretch while I show them what to do," Miss Carina said.

The other four girls moved to the back of the room, grabbed their water bottles and sat on the floor.

"We start at stage left," Miss Carina said. "It will take sixteen counts to move from here to the other end of the stage."

"That should take six or seven classes to teach," Shira muttered into Jasmine's ear.

"Shira, no talking!" Miss Carina snapped. "Listen!"

Jasmine bit her lip to keep from smiling at Shira's words.

"First step is a half turn, then a leap onto your right foot, with your left foot pointed, turned out and six inches off the ground. Bend at the waist, scoop your hands down and out over your leg, then stretch them out straight, reaching beyond your foot. Your head follows your hands. That's count one."

Jasmine's head swam as she tried to keep up with Miss Carina's rapid-fire instructions. She watched her teacher do the move twice and then attempted to copy it.

"Turn your foot out, Jasmine."

They did it again.

"Right, you'll have time to practice later. We need to keep going. From there, keep your left leg in the air, bend it, and swing it around behind you. Way behind you, into a lunge."

Jasmine did as she was told, hopping on her right foot to keep her balance. As she did so, she became aware of whispering and giggling behind her. The four girls who were supposed to be stretching were watching them closely. Melanie and Felicity had their heads together.

Jasmine wondered what they were talking about. Had they noticed that she was having a hard time keeping up with Miss Carina's instructions? Usually the girls clapped or cheered encouragement when one small group finished a combination of moves. Since the last competition, that didn't happen anymore.

"Jasmine, keep up. You missed the arms entirely. They need to swing around your head while your leg swings. And look up, not at the ground."

There was another giggle. They were definitely laughing at her.

"Next step," Miss Carina said.

Jasmine sighed. She still didn't understand the first two moves. At least Chelsea and Shira were in her group. They could help her figure it out later.

"Here, you'll be meeting the woodland creatures. First you're surprised, then you're angry. You push off your right foot, turn, come to relevé on your left and stop like you are preparing for a pirouette, with your right toe at your knee. Hold it for a count with your arms at your sides. You'll need to engage your core muscles or you'll fall out of it. I want to see a look of surprise on your face." Miss Carina demonstrated, pushing out of her lunge, spinning and coming to a complete stop in the other direction while balancing on the ball of one foot. She made it look easy.

Jasmine tried and promptly fell too far forward. The next time, she put less force into it and didn't make it to relevé.

"Last move for you today," Miss Carina said. "After you've held that for a full count, you're going to lunge forward onto your right foot, making a straight line from your head to your left foot. Now you're mad. I want you to look fierce." She demonstrated, her features so enraged that Jasmine took a step back, and then stood up, her face back to its normal, stern-looking self. "Any questions?"

Jasmine had about a million, but she didn't know where to start.

"Go to the corner of the room and practice while I work with the other group." She waved to the girls who were supposedly stretching. "Come on, girls, your turn."

"I'm so dead!" Jasmine said as they walked to the corner of the studio. "I've already forgotten the first step!"

"We'll figure it out," Shira said.

"Yeah, we'll help you," Chelsea said. "I want to show those other girls how good we are."

"You mean InMotion?" Jasmine asked.

Chelsea snorted. "No! I mean them." She pointed to the girls who were working with Miss Carina. Melanie saw her and smirked.

"Didn't you hear them making comments about us the whole time we were dancing?" Darveet asked.

"Yeah, who do they think they are?" Chelsea said.

Jasmine bit her lip. "Shouldn't we be a good example and not worry about them, just focus on ourselves?" She paused, wondering if the other girls would turn on her for what she'd said.

"That's what we're going to do," Chelsea said. "Focus on ourselves so we can be better."

"C'mon," Shira said. "Let's get going."

They reviewed the steps. Between them, they thought they remembered most of it. They ran through it. Every time they got to the relevé, Jasmine lost her balance in one direction or the other.

"This move is impossible!" she said.

"Keep trying," Darveet said. "You'll get it. Are you holding in your core muscles?"

"I think so." Jasmine didn't really know.

"Stop for a sec," Darveet said.

Jasmine stopped dancing and faced Darveet.

"Say *ha* really forcefully, like you're in karate."

"Ha!" Jasmine shouted. The girls who were working with Miss Carina stopped dancing and turned to look at her.

Darveet ignored them. "Did you feel how your muscles tightened?"

Jasmine nodded.

"Those are the muscles you have to keep tight while going up onto the ball of your foot. Without saying *ha*, of course."

Jasmine tried tightening the muscles without saying *ha*. She could do it if she thought the word in her head and breathed out a little bit.

"Thanks, Darveet," she said. "That works." Why hadn't Miss Carina ever shown her that trick?

"Let's put it all together," Miss Carina called out.

"Oh no," Jasmine whispered. "I still haven't got it."

"Don't worry," Shira said. "It'll be fine."

Miss Carina motioned them over to the far corner of the room. "We'll be in partners for this move once again. I want Darveet and Robyn at the front of the stage. Darveet, you'll start right in the corner. Robyn, you'll be about five steps away from her." The girls ran to their spots.

"Chelsea and Melanie, you'll be the next pair."

Someone gasped. There was an awkward silence while everyone waited to see what would happen. But the two girls just glared at each other and took their spots.

"Shira and Andrea, you're next, with Jasmine and Felicity at the back."

Jasmine thought the back was a good place for her on this sequence. Maybe nobody would notice if she tripped.

"Creatures, take your positions," Miss Carina said. The four girls crouched to the ground.

"And travelers, five, six, seven, eight."

Jasmine started her moves with the other three girls. Jump, stretch, lunge, relevé. As she wobbled on her relevé, trying to hold for a count, Felicity did a backward shoulder roll in front of her and came up onto her knees with her arms crossed in front of her forehead. Jasmine had to put her foot down before lunging forward over Felicity.

"Not bad. Do it again. Remember, travelers, you're supposed to look surprised when you are on relevé, then angry when you fall into the lunge. I should see the power coming through every pore."

They ran it again. Jasmine tried to feel surprised and angry, but mostly she worried about getting the steps right.

"Take a break," Miss Carina said. "I want you to watch Melanie and Chelsea. They showed me the emotion I want to see."

"No doubt," whispered Shira.

The girls sat in front of the mirror and watched Chelsea chase Melanie across the floor. Miss Carina was right. You could see the anger pulsating through Chelsea. Was Melanie supposed to look angry too? She certainly did.

For the rest of class, Miss Carina taught them the last count of eight for their partner work across the stage. By the end, Jasmine's head was reeling. She could barely keep the main steps right, let alone all the details for heads and fingers that Miss Carina was telling them.

As everyone got ready to go, Miss Carina called Jasmine over to her office. "I want to talk with you for a moment."

Jasmine walked over with a sinking heart. The muscles in her back squeezed into a giant knot.

Would Miss Carina say she wasn't good enough for the team?

"Come in," the teacher said.

Jasmine looked around the office, at the binders of information about ballet lessons and the schedules posted on every square inch of wall space. Her shoulders had climbed up around her ears. She forced herself to relax her muscles and drop her shoulders.

"You are a good technical dancer," Miss Carina said.

Jasmine's head snapped to her teacher. That was the last thing she'd expected to hear. "What?"

"You work hard, you're flexible, you listen well. I can tell that you're trying to get the steps exactly as I explain them."

Jasmine nodded. Wasn't that the point?

"That's all very important. But there's one thing that's missing."

Jasmine sighed. "I know. The emotion."

"That's what makes the difference between a good dancer and a great dancer. Especially in lyrical."

Jasmine nodded. "I'm trying, but I don't know how."

"I'm not sure that lyrical is the best type of dance for you."

Jasmine gasped. "You mean I'm off the team?"

Miss Carina shook her head. "Not at all. I couldn't rechoreograph the whole dance for seven people on such short notice. I mean that maybe next year you should try a different style of dance."

Jasmine blinked back tears. Why did her teacher have to start by getting her excited when really she was saying that she wasn't good enough for the team?

"In the meantime, keep trying to find the emotion. Dig deep. Draw on your experiences. I know you have that emotion inside you somewhere. Maybe you'll surprise me—and yourself—and figure out how to show it to the audience before the finals."

Jasmine nodded and backed out of the door, not able to say goodbye. She ran downstairs, passing Andrea and Darveet, who were still pulling on their sweaters. She was able to hold back the tears until she was in the street.

Six

Jasmine's mom was waiting for her in the car outside the studio. "What's wrong?" she asked as soon as Jasmine climbed into the passenger seat.

"Nothing."

"You're crying. It can't be nothing."

"I'm not good enough."

Her mom backed the car out of the parking spot. "Come on, honey. You're a great dancer. You wouldn't have made the team if you weren't. And you wouldn't have helped your team make it to the finals."

Jasmine sobbed. "Miss Carina told me I don't express enough emotion. That maybe I should try a different style of dance next year."

Her mom was quiet for a few moments. "She said that to you? With two weeks left to go before the competition? That's unacceptable."

Jasmine could hear the anger in her mom's voice. "She told me I'm a good technical dancer too." She didn't know why she felt the need to defend her teacher.

"That's good. But she still shouldn't have said anything about next year. Not right now. Do you want me to go talk to her?"

Jasmine shook her head so hard she thought it might fall off. If her mom talked to Miss Carina, that would make things ten times worse.

"I want to help," her mom said, her hands squeezing the steering wheel.

Jasmine sighed. "I know. I don't want to talk about it anymore."

Her mom nodded, and they rode the rest of the way home in silence.

* * *

That night Jasmine lay in bed staring at the ceiling, running the moves in her head.

"How's it going?" her mom asked when she poked her head in to say good night.

Jasmine shrugged and didn't say anything.

"I think you're a beautiful dancer, no matter what Miss Carina says."

"Thanks." She tried to smile but couldn't. "I'm thinking of quitting."

Her mom gasped. "What?"

"She's only keeping me on the team because it'll be hard for her to change the choreography. If she doesn't want me there, then I'm going to quit."

"But you worked so hard to get on the team! And you love dance so much."

"I used to love dance so much."

"Well, you know I'll support you whatever you do. I don't like to see you unhappy. And I do worry that you're working yourself too hard."

Jasmine sat up. "Really, you'd let me quit, just like that?"

Her mother nodded. "If it's what you want."

"You aren't even going to tell me that I'd be letting all my friends down if I quit? Or that I should try harder?"

"Do you want me to say those things?"

Jasmine flopped back on her pillow. "I can't believe you'd let me quit so easily!"

Her mother threw her hands in the air. "What do you want me to say? I'm trying to be supportive here."

"I don't know!" Jasmine squeezed her eyes shut, wishing her mom would leave but also wanting her comfort.

"Maybe you should go see your grandma. She's got lawn bowling tomorrow, but she'll be home on Thursday. She might be able to help."

Jasmine gave a small nod and rolled to face the wall. Her mom was right. Grandma Verbenka always helped her see things more clearly.

* * *

Her grandmother lived within walking distance of the Moondance studio, so Jasmine took the bus to her house after school on Thursday. She'd have time for a quick visit before dance practice.

Since the practice on Tuesday, she'd flip-flopped between wanting to quit and wanting to stay and show Miss Carina what she could do.

Maybe her teacher had been trying to get her to quit when she called her into the office. Was this another one of her mind games? Well, Jasmine would show her. Or not.

Maybe her grandmother would be able to tell her how to show her emotions. Nobody else had been able to teach her how. Certainly not Miss Carina. Wasn't that her teacher's job? Should she be kicking Jasmine off the team when it was really all her fault?

By the time Jasmine arrived at her grandmother's, she felt like there was a thundercloud building inside her.

Her grandmother's pencil-thin eyebrows shot up into her dyed-red hair when Jasmine walked in the door. "What the matter with you, *moya radost*?"

"Dance," Jasmine said, leaving her backpack by the door and giving her grandma a peck on the cheek. She smiled to herself at the irony of being called "my happiness." It was her grandmother's pet name for her, but it didn't exactly fit this afternoon.

"I should have known," her grandma said. "You look just like my mother."

"Huh?"

"Pardon."

"What?"

"You say *pardon*, not *huh* or *what*."

"Oh. Sorry. Pardon?"

"You know that your great-grandmother was ballet dancer?"

Jasmine nodded. "Mom always tells me that Great-Grandma would have been proud to see me dance."

Her grandma smiled and patted the couch beside her. "Dance genes skipped two generations."

"I'm not exactly her caliber," Jasmine said as she sat down. "Didn't she dance in St. Petersburg? At the Vaganova something?"

"She dance in St. Petersburg, yes. Now company is called Vaganova Academy of Russian Ballet. But back then city was called Leningrad, and ballet company called the Leningrad State Choreographic Institute. Is mouthful, no? When things weren't going well, she looked like you."

"When did you see her dance? I thought she had to leave the ballet when she was pregnant with you."

Her grandma shook her head. "Leave the company, yes. But not leave dance. She love it too much to stop. Always dance, dance, dance, no matter where she was." She pushed a plate of macaroons toward Jasmine. "Have some cookies."

Jasmine didn't like macaroons but knew her grandma would be offended if she didn't eat one. She took a cookie, then settled back into the couch. She'd heard stories about her great-grandmother before, but she always enjoyed hearing them again. "Tell me about her."

"She went back to teach at the ballet school when I was old enough. I go with her to class sometimes. That where I see her look like a storm cloud, like you, when things not going well."

Jasmine forced herself to take a small bite of macaroon.

"In 1950, we leave. Defect. Because my father is in danger. His best friend arrested as a spy for the west. My father is guilty by association. He and my mom think he will be sent to Siberia. So when the ballet travels to west to put on show, she brings us with her, and we escape."

Grandma Verbenka stared out the window, lost in thought. Jasmine wondered what memories she was reliving. She'd heard lots of stories from her mom about the hardships her great-grandparents had endured while defecting. They couldn't just walk away from the Soviet Union, but had had to escape, putting themselves and their friends and family who remained behind in great danger. What had it been like for her grandma to do that as a little girl?

With a start, her grandmother focused on Jasmine again. "When we get to Canada, my mother sad, sad, that she cannot dance in proper company. Too busy caring for me. But she decide to form group of Russian dancers that put on a show for people from old country. They dance for fun, not a professional company."

Her grandmother pointed to a photo leaning against the window. "Bring that here."

Jasmine stood up and brought it over.

"This is her with Russian friends in Toronto," her grandmother said.

Jasmine peered at the photo she'd seen so many times before. Her great-grandmother stood in the middle of a small group of women dressed in shabby gray dresses. They were all tall and thin and held their backs straight and their chins high.

"Not matter that she getting older, that not proper stage, that everybody dressed in old, simple clothes. When she dance, she doesn't think about audience. Doesn't think about moves she practice, practice, practice. She say her body know what to do already. When she go onstage to perform, all she think about is the feeling of the dance."

Jasmine groaned. That word again. *Feeling*.

"What wrong? Are you sick?" Her grandmother sat forward and placed a hand on Jasmine's forehead.

"I'm not sick. But I'm thinking of quitting dance."

Her grandma gasped. "You! But you dance always! I remember you as little girl, twirling through my *tchotckes*. I was sure you knock them all over. Don't you remember all the hours you and your little friends spend making dances in the basement?"

Jasmine did remember that. She and her girlfriends had spent whole afternoons choreographing dances based on moves they made up.

Sometimes they had music, and sometimes they sang along.

"Dance isn't fun anymore though."

Her grandma nodded. "Dance is work. That what your great-grandmother say."

"So you don't think I should quit?"

"That your decision, not mine. But don't quit because is hard. Quit only if you don't want to do it anymore."

Jasmine paused. Did she still want to dance? Her grandma always had a way of getting to the important stuff. Really, that was all that mattered. Did she still want to dance? Yes.

"What time is class today?" her grandma asked.

"It starts at four."

"Is five minutes to four."

Jasmine gasped. "Oh no!" She jumped off the couch and ran for the door, then ran back and gave her grandma a kiss on the cheek. "Thanks."

Her grandma nodded and shooed her away. "Run! Don't be late!"

She was late. She arrived at five minutes after four, and she didn't have her leotard on yet.

Miss Carina's face darkened when Jasmine walked in the door. The warm-up had already started. "One hundred crunches!" she barked. "Twenty for each minute."

Melanie and Felicity giggled.

Jasmine dropped her bag and glared at them, then lay down on the floor to start her crunches. A hundred was over the top. She'd only been five minutes late. But even worse was having her supposed friends laugh at her. Maybe she *should* have quit.

After fifty crunches her muscles started to feel tired, and she was breathing hard. By seventy she had slowed down. At the end of a hundred, her muscles were screaming and sweat was dripping off her.

She took her place in the warm-up. Miss Carina ignored her as she got ready for the kick sequence. Shira smiled and mouthed, "You did it!"

Jasmine tried to smile back, but she was too tired.

As she did her battements, she could feel herself getting more and more angry. Miss Carina had it in for her. Melanie and Felicity were so mean. Hadn't they ever been late to class?

She was tempted to quit right then and there. But that would give all three of them what they wanted. No, she'd show them. She'd stick with it.

"Point your toes, Jasmine," Miss Carina called out.

"Straight legs, Jasmine—I've told you a hundred times."

With each comment, Jasmine said nothing, as anger boiled inside her.

Finally, the warm-up was over. "We're going to start with the traveling scene again," Miss Carina said.

Great. The part she found hardest.

As they lined up with their partners, Felicity whispered to her, "Have fun doing crunches? Why were you late? Hanging out with Will?"

Jasmine had to hold her hands behind her back to stop herself from reaching out and shoving her.

"Five, six, seven, eight," Miss Carina called.

Jasmine wasn't sure if she remembered the steps. But she could hardly think about them anyway. Mostly she was thinking about how mad she was at Felicity. All of that anger went into her steps. The best part was when she got to lunge over her. It was so tempting to spit.

Miss Carina cut the music. "Jasmine!"

Jasmine turned. What now? She was so tired of being singled out. She knew she couldn't dance as well as everyone else. Was Miss Carina going to let the class know too?

"You did it! That was the best I've ever seen you dance! So much emotion! So much anger!"

Jasmine could feel her mouth dropping open. "But I was hardly thinking about the moves at all," she admitted.

"That's what I've been trying to tell you! Don't think about the moves. Your body knows what to do. Think about the feeling!"

"Uh-huh." Jasmine couldn't believe this was happening. She'd been so distracted and angry that she'd danced better than ever?

Miss Carina stared at her without talking for a moment. Jasmine's tired muscles started to cramp with nervousness. What had she done wrong now?

Her teacher crooked a finger at her. "I'm moving you to the front."

Seven

Miss Carina pointed to Chelsea and Melanie. "Switch places with Jasmine and Felicity."

Jasmine tried not to meet Chelsea's eyes as she passed her. Instead, she focused on feeling happy. She'd done it! She'd proven to Miss Carina that she did know how to dance. She was worthy of being on the team.

But now that she wasn't so angry, would she be able to dance so well?

"Run that section again," Miss Carina said.

Jasmine took a deep breath. She couldn't blow this or she'd be sent to the back again. *Think.* What had she done? She'd been angry. She hadn't thought so much about the moves.

So she had to feel angry again. Her eyes scanned the room. Chelsea and Darveet were whispering to each other and looking her way. Jasmine's cheeks flushed. *That wasn't so hard.* Now she had to hold on to the feeling.

The music started. Jasmine's mind began to kick in. *Jump. Point your toe more.* She pushed the thoughts to the back of her mind and focused on how angry she was instead.

"Good," Miss Carina said. "Let's run it from the top."

Doing the dance from the top proved to be harder than doing the part they'd just done. Jasmine didn't need to be angry at the start; she needed to be happy. Finding something to be happy about right now was difficult.

When did she feel happy? She thought about the feeling she had every week at the start of warm-up, when they did their pliés and breathing. She imagined she was doing that exercise as she did the opening moves of the dance.

It worked. She felt light and happy, and she thought her body might look that way too. Dancing was more interesting this way.

"Nice, Jasmine," Miss Carina said. "Melanie, you're rushing."

Jasmine faltered for a moment as she prepared for her chaînés. The look on Melanie's face was evil. And it was all directed at Jasmine.

"Ignore Melanie," Shira whispered after they'd run the number again. "She's jealous." Her friend gave her a squeeze on the arm. "You did it!"

Jasmine smiled and nodded. At least one other person in the room was happy for her.

"Let's move on to the next section. We're nearing the end of the dance," Miss Carina said.

"It's about time," Shira muttered. "We only have a week left."

"No kidding," Jasmine said. "She's leaving it so late."

"I'd like to finish the ending today," Miss Carina continued. "We have an extra two-hour practice on Saturday. We can clean it then, and that will leave us with two practices next week to polish it up."

Jasmine had forgotten about the Saturday practice. She didn't really want to spend her weekend in the stuffy dance studio, but it was better than feeling unprepared for the competition.

"The most serious part of our story comes when the traveler arrives at her destination only to find that she has no friends, and no one wants to approach her because she's so angry."

"This story's quite the downer, isn't it?" Shira said.

Miss Carina pursed her lips at Shira's interruption. "As you know, it gets better. One girl is brave enough to approach her. As soon as she makes one friend, her anger falls away, and everyone else is happy to talk to her too."

Jasmine wondered how the audience would figure all this out. Sometimes the dancers were the girl, sometimes they were woodland creatures, sometimes they were family, and sometimes they were friends in the new town. She guessed it wasn't supposed to be taken too literally. Would anybody in the audience get it though?

"For the part where she is shunned, I want one person to play the traveler, one to play the girl who befriends her, and everyone else will be the townspeople."

The girls had been taking a break and stretching while Miss Carina spoke. At her latest words, all eight of them sat up. Somebody's water bottle clattered to the floor. Their teacher was announcing a duet. This differed significantly from the original dance.

Miss Carina's eyes roamed over the eight of them, weighing her options. "Right. Shira, come here. You can play the friend."

Jasmine smiled. Shira had never been singled out for anything other than mouthing off, yet she was a beautiful dancer. Putting emotion into her moves had never been a problem for her.

"And for the traveler..." Miss Carina paused and eyed everyone again. Jasmine felt like an orphan pup waiting to be taken home from the animal shelter. "Jasmine."

Jasmine bolted to her feet. She'd known Miss Carina had been happy with her dancing, but happy enough to earn Jasmine a duet?

"I'm going to teach the rest of the group their part first. You two might as well learn it, but stand to the side so that I can work on the spacing."

Shira grabbed Jasmine's arm and dragged her to the side of the studio. It was a good thing too, because Jasmine was so stunned she could hardly understand Miss Carina's words.

"This is so awesome!" Shira said.

"I'm glad it's the two of us." As Jasmine spoke, she saw Melanie and Chelsea looking daggers at them. She was doubly glad to have Shira beside her.

Jasmine tried to follow along as Miss Carina taught the class an entirely new sequence of steps, but her head wasn't really in it. She was too excited about having a duet and too worried about what this was going to mean for her friendship with the rest of the team.

How had this happened to them? In the past, they had all worked together. It didn't used to matter so much who was at the front, or who had a solo. Was it all because of the competition with InMotion?

After Miss Carina had finished with the larger group, she called Jasmine and Shira over to learn their parts. "I want you two to come for an extra practice on Saturday, before everyone else."

Jasmine nodded. She could do that. Not that Miss Carina was *asking*. She assumed that her students were always at her beck and call.

"We'll block it out today, and then we'll go through the fine-tuning on Saturday." Miss Carina showed them what they had to do. It started with

Jasmine raging alone in the middle of the stage while Shira slowly approached her, tapped her on the shoulder and mimed asking to be friends.

Jasmine's eyes widened as she watched Miss Carina. Her part of the dance was fast and difficult. It involved a lot of whipping herself around, with a few back rolls and laybacks thrown in.

After Shira approached her, things got easier. They spun around together, holding on to each other's arms, which looked like fun, and then they ran around the circle of townspeople, as though Shira was introducing Jasmine to all of them.

"I don't expect you to remember all of the steps today."

That's good, Jasmine thought, *since you haven't taught them to us yet.*

Miss Carina called the rest of the team back to the center of the room. "Run through the part I taught you a few minutes ago so that you all get your spacing down. Start with the ending pose of the traveling section when you are in your partners, go through the section when you dance around Shira and Jasmine, and finish with the two of them running around you."

Jasmine went to the far right front of the stage where she and Felicity were to finish the partner work.

Felicity stood with her arms crossed, waiting for Jasmine. "You sure you can handle the spotlight?"

Jasmine took a step back from her. "Yeah." She wasn't sure at all, but she wasn't about to give Felicity the pleasure of hearing her say it.

"It's impressive that she chose you, it being your first year on the team and all."

Jasmine shrugged.

"All I'm saying is, you'd think she'd have chosen someone who'd put in the years of work."

"It's only a ten-second part, Felicity. It's not like I'm playing the Sugar Plum Fairy or anything."

Felicity sniffed.

"Five, six, seven, eight," Miss Carina called.

The girls jazz-ran into their next formation. Jasmine moved to the center of the stage and curled herself into a ball. That was about all she remembered from Miss Carina's demonstration. That and a back roll. She tried to do one while everyone else danced their moves, but she got stuck halfway through it. Shira came to tap her on the shoulder, and she had to scramble to her feet.

They hugged. Then they tried the spinning move, but their arms slipped apart and they landed on their butts. Shira started to laugh.

"Girls! Stop!"

Everyone stopped.

"What was that?" Miss Carina was looking at Jasmine and Shira, furious.

"Um, we were trying to do what you did," Shira said.

"Well, don't. You're wasting everyone's time. I'll teach it to you on the weekend. Just stand there for now."

Jasmine bowed her head. Her cheeks flushed. So much for trying to keep up. She could feel the eyes of all the dancers on her and was sure they were asking the same question she was. Why had Miss Carina picked her, the worst dancer on the team?

They ran it again. This time, Jasmine didn't try to remember any of the moves. She just stood there, feeling like a dork, until Shira tapped her on the shoulder and pulled her by the arm and they ran around the circle.

"Better. Let's move on to the ending."

Finally. They were at the end. They had three classes left after this one. Three classes for her to learn the steps well enough that she could forget them and focus on the emotions of the dance.

"I haven't decided if this is what the ending will be exactly," Miss Carina said, "but we'll give it a try."

Jasmine pressed her fingers to the bridge of her nose. How many times was Miss Carina going to change the dance?

"We'll keep the last move the same, with the group layback. The judges liked that. And we'll finish with the same ending pose."

Jasmine nodded. That was good. Even though the layback hurt and was hard to do, at least it was a move they all knew.

"Before that, you're all going to dance together, in a staggered line across the stage."

More good news. Nobody had to fight for the front spot if they were in a staggered line.

"This is a celebration," Miss Carina said. "It should be happy and exciting. It's also our chance to wow the judges. Jasmine and Shira, you'll lead the circle into a line. You've already run around the inside of the circle. Now, go through the space between Robyn and Darveet and to the left side of the stage. Everyone else follow. Space yourselves out."

They did as Miss Carina said. "Like that, but move the line farther back."

Everybody shuffled back.

"We're going to do a turning sequence. Triple pirouette, double chaînés, then an axel."

Jasmine could barely do a triple pirouette. And she hated axels. They involved doing chaînés, then jumping off one foot, doing a full turn in the air and landing on the same foot. As if that wasn't hard enough, you had to tuck both feet up to your butt and whirl your arm around your head at the same time. Jasmine could never get all the pieces together.

"Try it," Miss Carina said.

They ran through the sequence.

"Jasmine, you're slow on your pirouette, and you didn't tuck your legs on the axel. Try it again."

The next time, Jasmine finished her triple pirouette, but she was so dizzy she almost ran into Melanie on the axel.

"Watch it!" Melanie said.

"Sorry!"

"One more time," Miss Carina said.

They did it over and over. Miss Carina was never satisfied, and they still had ten seconds of dance to choreograph before the final move.

When class time was up, Miss Carina said, "We'll have to stop there for today. I'll see you Saturday. I want you all to practice the choreography we learned today so that I don't have to reteach anything on the weekend."

Everybody nodded and headed for their water bottles and clothes.

"You better practice those triples, Jasmine," Felicity said. "We don't want you to make any mistakes in the competition."

Shira jumped in before Jasmine could say anything. "You're the one who made all the mistakes in the last competition! You told us so yourself!"

"It's okay, Shira," Jasmine said. "I do need to practice my triples. And my axels." She looked straight at Felicity. "I always practice. I always worry about being the one that will let down the team."

Felicity dropped her eyes to the floor. "Good," she mumbled, then grabbed her things and ran down the stairs.

"How can you be so calm and nice when she's so awful?" Shira asked as they walked out a few minutes later.

Jasmine shrugged. "We used to be a team. I want us to be one again."

Eight

On Friday, Jasmine sat slumped in her chair, waiting for homeroom to start. Will came in and stopped at her desk.

"What's up? You look miserable," he said. "Dance?"

Jasmine sighed. "Yeah. Miss Carina moved me to the front and gave me a duet with Shira."

Will's forehead wrinkled. "But that's what you've always wanted! What's the problem?"

"The problem is that I got what I've always wanted, and it sucks. Miss Carina picks on me all the time, she's giving me harder and harder stuff to do, and the only person on the team who's still nice to me is Shira."

Will smirked. "It's lonely at the top."

Jasmine sat up in her desk. "I'm serious! I don't even know why Miss Carina picked me! I danced well once, and she seems to think that means I'm some amazing dancer. But now I can't keep up. I'm going to let the whole team down."

"No, you're not. Why don't we go to the drama room at lunch and you can practice with me?"

"You'd do that?"

"Of course."

Jasmine smiled for the first time since the practice the night before. "Thanks."

*   *   *

After math class, she went to find Will. As she neared the drama room, she heard music with a heavy drumbeat blasting from inside. She opened the door a crack and saw Will dancing by himself, unaware that she was watching him.

She cracked the door open another few inches. He didn't seem to be practicing a set routine— he was just goofing around, trying out moves. He jumped, crossed his legs, spun in a circle to uncross them, then took a wide step to the right and dragged his left foot across the floor before stepping together with a pop of his upper body.

Jasmine pushed the door open farther and strutted toward him, doing her best imitation of a hip-hop dancer, bent over toward the floor and bouncing to the lyrics.

Will looked up in surprise, then smiled and grabbed her hands, pulling her into the dance. They faced each other, snaking their shoulders and ribs back and forth in opposite directions. On the last beats of the music, they came face to face in the center of the room. Will reached around and gripped Jasmine in the small of her back and stepped toward her. Jasmine fell back onto his hand in a layback as the music ended.

"I feel like I'm doing the tango or something!" Jasmine laughed as Will pulled her back up to standing.

"Not quite the same beat," Will said, his green eyes staring at her from inches away.

Jasmine swallowed and twirled out of his arms. "Thanks for helping me with this. Wanna see my moves?"

"Yeah. I always want to see your moves."

Jasmine felt herself blush. Did Will mean something more than that? No, he was just Will, and he always would be. She showed him the choreography they'd worked on the day before.

"Not bad," Will said. "But you need to work on your triple."

"I know! That's why I'm here."

"I thought you weren't supposed to do stuff like that in lyrical anyway," Will said.

"So did I," Jasmine said. "But Miss Carina wants to make the dance flashier and more difficult."

"I don't think you're getting enough power from your preparation," Will said. "Try doing a deeper plié."

Jasmine pliéd more deeply.

"No, even deeper."

"But I feel like I'm in some kind of squat. It must look ridiculous."

"Doesn't. And it's what will get you around three times. Trust me."

"How do you know about pirouettes?"

"I told you, I used to take ballet when I was younger. Besides, we turn in hip-hop. Just not up on our toes and all pretty." He popped up onto the ball of his foot and waved his arms around like an octopus dancing.

Jasmine giggled and fell out of her plié. "Stop! That's not what we look like!"

"Oh, sorry." He sucked in his cheeks and straightened his back. "Is this more like it?"

Jasmine laughed again. "Better."

"Then show me your triple."

Jasmine pliéd so deeply she thought she might drop to the ground, then popped up, straightening her supporting leg, tightening her core muscles and whipping her head around. Once. Twice. Three times.

"You did it!" Will called. "That was way better!"

Jasmine stopped to center herself. "It worked! You're amazing!" She lunged toward him to give him a hug, then reached up a hand for a high five instead. "You sure you won't join our team?"

Will shook his head. "We've been through this before. Besides, I don't dance to compete. I dance because I love it."

"You can compete and love dance," Jasmine said.

"Doesn't sound to me like you're loving it," Will said.

Jasmine turned away from Will and started chewing on her thumbnail. He was right. But she'd already decided that she was going to see it through to the end of the competition. And she had felt that love for dance, especially when she'd been too angry to think about the steps.

She needed to find a way to make her group a team again and enjoy dance at the same time.

*　*　*

The next day, Jasmine was no closer to solving that problem by the end of her extra practice with Shira. They lay stretched out on the floor, resting for a few moments before the second part of rehearsal began. Miss Carina was in her office. They had spent an intense two hours with her, learning their parts. Jasmine's head was reeling, and her body ached.

The door opened and Melanie came in.

"Hi, Melanie," Jasmine called.

Melanie nodded to them but didn't say anything.

"Here we go again," Shira said.

Miss Carina came out of her office, her face pinched and pale. "Where is everybody?"

"It's only five to eleven," Shira said.

The door opened, and the rest of the team filed in.

"Girls, move it. The clock is ticking. We need to get this dance finished."

The girls put their stuff down and moved into the studio, still chatting.

"Faster!" Miss Carina said. "And no talking today. We need to get down to business!"

The talking stopped immediately. Jasmine and Shira jumped up to join the group.

Jasmine grimaced. It hadn't exactly been fun spending two hours almost alone with Miss Carina, but she hadn't been this mean.

"I want to get the dance finished today, so that we have one class to clean it and a final rehearsal before the competition. No wasting time. Got it?"

Everyone nodded.

"Right. I'm assuming you've all practiced your partner work, so we'll move right into the ending sequence. Show me your triples into axels again."

They formed their line, Miss Carina counted them in, and they did their triple pirouettes and their axels.

Miss Carina nodded. "Okay. I can live with that. Jasmine, you still need to tuck your foot more on your axel."

Jasmine's cheeks burned. Couldn't Miss Carina at least say something nice about her pirouette?

"We only have three bars of music to finish before you go into your layback together. This is the celebration sequence. I want it to be happy, and to be something that you all do together. I have an idea, but I need to see what it looks like first." She stared at them, one after the other. It looked like she was doing calculations in her head. "Make a circle."

"Hasn't she ever heard of the word *please*?" Shira muttered in Jasmine's ear as they moved into a circle.

"Shira!" Miss Carina said. "I said, no talking, no wasting time! Get into the circle or you'll be doing crunches later!"

Shira flinched beside Jasmine. Jasmine gave her hand a squeeze.

"Stand shoulder to shoulder," Miss Carina said. "Thread your arms behind the person beside you. Now grab the hand of the next person over on either side."

It took them awhile to figure that one ⟨
eventually all the dancers were holding ha⟨

"Now, chassé to the right."

They started to move slowly to the right, but
each girl kept tripping on the feet of the dancer
next to her.

"Ouch!" Darveet called out. "You stepped on
me!"

"Sorry," Shira said. "Hey, Felicity, you kicked
me."

"Girls!" Miss Carina shouted. "Watch where
you put your feet."

"But our legs are too close together," Melanie
said. "We can't help it."

"Stop," Miss Carina said.

The girls came to a standstill with much
jostling of shoulders.

"We'll try something else. Drop your hands."
Everybody did as she instructed. "Turn and
face outward. Now put your right hand on the
shoulder of the person next to you."

Jasmine put her hand on Felicity's shoulder.
Shira put her hand on Jasmine's.

"Now," said Miss Carina. "I want you to
do the grapevine step in a circle. Step right,

behind with your left, step right, in front with your left."

The girls moved in a circle, doing the grapevine.

"I'm pretty sure I did this dance at my cousin's wedding last month," Shira said.

Jasmine held back her giggle. This was the big showy ending Miss Carina was looking for?

"Stop!" Miss Carina called.

What now?

"I don't like it," Miss Carina said. "We're going to try something else."

The afternoon dragged on. By the end of the day, they'd tried four more endings, and Miss Carina wasn't happy with any of them.

"Class dismissed," she said. "We'll finish it and clean it on Tuesday."

"What a waste of time," Shira said as they pulled on their hoodies and sweatpants.

"Don't let her hear you say that," Jasmine whispered, "or she'll flip."

"She can't make me do crunches now that class is over," Shira said.

"I wouldn't bet on it."

Nine

On Tuesday, Miss Carina greeted the girls at the door by saying, "No warm-up today."

"Hi, Miss Carina," Shira said.

The teacher gave Shira a confused look. She had completely missed the sarcasm in Shira's voice.

"We have to finish the dance today," Miss Carina said.

Jasmine tried not to roll her eyes. They'd heard that one before. They were supposed to be cleaning the dance today, not finishing it. Why couldn't Miss Carina pick an ending and stick with it?

"Get into your circle," the teacher said.

For some reason, it really grated on Jasmine that Miss Carina never said please. Did she think they didn't deserve to be treated with any respect? Didn't she understand that they might work harder if they got praised occasionally? Jasmine knew Miss Carina was stressed about getting the dance finished, but didn't she also realize that the girls deserved to be treated nicely once in a while?

The girls moved into their circle. Melanie made a point of turning her back to Jasmine and Shira. Would she never give it up? Exactly what had Jasmine done to her? Nothing, other than being chosen by the teacher to play a role in the dance. How childish to be so jealous for so long. Jasmine looked away from Melanie. She didn't want to give Melanie the satisfaction of knowing she was bothered by the nasty looks.

"We're going back to the original idea of moving in a circle," Miss Carina said.

"But that didn't work!" Shira said.

"Shira!" Miss Carina screamed. "I have told you hundreds of times not to talk back. Show respect for your teacher!"

For the first time ever, Shira looked affected by Miss Carina's words. Her face flushed and she shrank back, taking a step out of the circle.

Jasmine could understand why. Miss Carina's whole body was rigid and leaning aggressively over Shira. Something inside Jasmine snapped and she said, "If you want respect, then why don't you treat *us* with respect instead of yelling at us like we're a bunch of dogs? In fact, I wouldn't treat my dog the way you treat us!"

There was a collective gasp from the circle. Jasmine gulped. She stood frozen, horrified by what she'd said. Should she run away now?

Miss Carina stared at her with an open mouth. Jasmine waited for her to blow. Surely she was going to kick her off the team.

Miss Carina took a deep breath. Jasmine held hers. She could feel her cheeks burning. It looked as if her teacher was gearing up for the scream of a lifetime. But then Miss Carina let her breath out again. "Fine," she said in a surprisingly calm voice. "If you think you can do a better job, you finish the dance." And then she spun around, strode to her office and slammed the door.

There was a moment of stunned silence as the girls looked at each other. And then chaos erupted.

"Nice work, Jasmine. Now we only have two classes left, no dance and no teacher," Melanie said.

"I can't believe you said that to her!" Felicity said.

Darveet pressed her hand to her forehead. "What are we going to do?"

"Thanks for standing up for me," Shira said. She squeezed Jasmine's hand.

Chelsea clapped her hands in a way that sounded eerily like Miss Carina's. "We need to get going on our routine. We're running out of time. What should we do?"

"Let's try the circle again," Robyn said. "Miss Carina thought we could make it work."

Chelsea nodded. "Okay. Everyone hold hands the way she showed us."

They did as Chelsea told them.

"Now chassé to the right."

They tried to chassé, but they had the same problem as before. They all banged into each other.

Robyn fell to the floor. "Shira, you pushed me!"

"No, I didn't!" Shira said. "You banged into me and fell!"

Robyn got up and stood face to face with Shira. "Don't stick your foot out so far!"

Chelsea clapped her hands. "Let's try it again."

"No!" Shira said. "This move doesn't work."

"Well, what else do you suggest?" Chelsea asked. "You some kind of choreographer or something?"

"I'm sure I can come up with something," Shira said. "Who said you got to be in charge anyway?"

"Nobody did, but we need to figure it out," Chelsea said. She looked at Jasmine and added, "Since you chased our teacher away."

Jasmine stepped forward. "All I did was tell her what she needed to hear. She's been treating us like dirt all week. Who can say they've enjoyed class?"

There was silence.

"And doesn't anybody else care that our team has completely fallen apart?"

Again there was silence.

Finally, Robyn stepped forward. "I care. We used to like each other."

Jasmine nodded. "Exactly. We used to work together. I used to love coming to dance. But for the last few weeks, the only reason I've come is so I could prove that I wasn't going to quit."

"It's true," Felicity said. "Class hasn't been any fun lately. It's all Miss Carina's fault."

"No, it isn't," Jasmine said. "It's mostly our fault. We're the ones who are being so awful to each other. We're never going to beat InMotion if we can't even get along as a team."

"Or if our number isn't finished," Chelsea said. "Why don't you finish it, if you're so smart?"

So much for being a team, Jasmine thought. "Fine. I will." She looked around the circle.

"What are you waiting for?" Chelsea asked. "Tell us what to do."

"I'm thinking," Jasmine said. "I need to know what to do first. Why don't you all take a break? Have some water."

"Yes, Miss Carina," Darveet said. But at least she had a smile on her face and not a sneer.

Jasmine walked over to the corner and closed her eyes. She figured she had about two minutes to figure this out before she lost her chance and they started bickering again. *Think.* It needed to be something that was a celebration and not too hard for them to figure out in such a short time, but also something that would make them all feel like a team again.

She thought back to being a little kid, dancing with her friends. What had she loved about dance back then? Being with friends. Listening to music. Creating new steps.

When had she last loved dance? When she was goofing around with Will.

What if they all did whatever made them happiest? Someone could do a split leap. Someone else a pirouette.

Except this celebration was about everyone working together.

"I've got it!" Jasmine called.

The other members of the team were in the corner of the studio, stretching, talking or drinking from their water bottles. The whispering petered out as they looked over at her.

"Come get in line where we were after the triple pirouettes and axels," Jasmine said. "Please."

The girls stood up, put their bottles down and sauntered over. Jasmine was dying to tell them to hurry but decided to keep her mouth shut.

"This part of the dance is supposed to be a celebration, right?"

Chelsea nodded.

"I think when we celebrate we should do something that makes us feel good," Jasmine said.

"Meaning what?" Robyn asked.

"Well, that's just it. We probably all have a favorite move, right? I mean, Chelsea, you have the most amazing split leaps, and Shira, you used to be a gymnast and you can do side aerials."

Both girls smiled.

"That's what I mean!" Jasmine said, almost jumping up and down. "I want us all to do something that makes us happy!"

Chelsea and Shira looked at each other. They saw the grins on each other's faces and burst out laughing.

"Everybody, think of one move you can do that makes you smile. It doesn't have to be fancy or hard."

There was a moment of silence as the girls thought, then an eruption of noise.

"Sissonne!"

"Chaînés!"

"Double pirouette."

"Okay, okay!" Jasmine said. "I think you've all got the idea. The timing should work perfectly if we finish our axels, then move down the line, with everyone doing their move one after the other. As soon as you're done, jazz-run behind the line and start a really big circle."

The girls were all nodding, clearly liking the idea. Jasmine felt a shiver of excitement. They were working like a team again. Nobody was bickering. And it had all been her idea. If only Miss Carina were here to see it.

She counted them in. "Five, six, seven, eight." Darveet, who was farthest left, started with a straddle jump. Jasmine was amazed at how high she could go. It looked like her legs were beside her ears.

As soon as she landed, Shira did an aerial. Then Felicity did a double pirouette, Chelsea a split leap, Robyn some chaînés. It was Jasmine's turn. She leaped into the air, throwing her head back and tucking her legs behind her. She didn't know what the move was called, but she'd been practicing it all her life, ever since she'd seen it done in *The Lion King* musical when she was five. She ran to her spot in the circle, followed by Melanie.

"That was so much fun!" Melanie said.

Felicity nodded. "I think we need to work on our timing, but this can definitely work."

"Let's try it with the music," Jasmine said. "Let's start with the axels this time."

They ran back to their spots. Jasmine's heart was pounding, but not from exertion. She was so excited. It felt like she was back in grade one, making up dances with her friends.

She found the right spot in the music and counted them in again. They did their pirouettes and axels, then began their celebration moves, as Jasmine had started calling them in her head. With the music, they were able to keep their timing. When Melanie arrived in the circle, Jasmine ran to turn off the music.

"Hey," Chelsea called. "We're only a few beats away from the layback."

"Normally, we're facing out before the layback," Melanie said. "Should we turn around?"

Jasmine paused. Melanie was looking at her for direction. She took a deep breath. She didn't want to wreck the moment. "No. But we need to do something for three counts before we walk together."

"Let's hold hands in the circle," Shira said.

Robyn groaned. "Not that move again!"

Everybody laughed.

"Shira's right," Jasmine said. "We won't go as close together as we did with Miss Carina. Take only one step forward." Everybody did, making the circle a bit smaller. "Hold hands." She was about to tell everyone to chassé in a circle but realized that that would really look like they were in baby ballet. There was a reason Miss Carina had told them to link arms behind each other, even if it hadn't worked. They needed two beats of doing something with their arms linked.

"I need to listen to the music again," Jasmine said. She let go of Melanie's and Robyn's hands and pressed *Play*. She listened hard to the words and the beat. "When we get to this circle, she's talking about belonging. And the music slows down for a bit before it rises again on the layback."

"Why don't we sway?" Robyn suggested.

Swaying wasn't very fancy. Jasmine was about to shoot down the idea. But then she remembered how everyone had given her a chance. Besides, swaying could look pretty. "Sure, let's try it. Left first, for one count each."

They grasped hands again and swayed left and right.

"That's not bad," Melanie said. "What if we exaggerate it a bit more, tip our heads to the side and fully transfer our weight?"

Jasmine nodded. She'd been thinking the same thing. For once, Melanie was working with the group. "Let's try it again and go right into our layback."

They did it again. Melanie was right. The swaying looked better that way. Jasmine stepped forward two steps and grasped Chelsea's arm across the circle. They smiled at each other before leaning backward and making their sunflower shape.

Everyone came back up with no falls.

"We rock!" Shira said into the circle. The girls burst into laughter as they raised their arms and then fell onto the floor.

They jumped up and ran to their final pose. "It works!" Jasmine cried. "We're finished!"

"Let's run it from the top," Chel.

Jasmine nodded. When all the
in their opening spots, she started
and sprinted for her place. They ran t
number. It was strange doing it without Miss
Carina calling instructions to them. They weren't
perfect, but they made it through the whole piece,
including the new section Jasmine had choreo-
graphed, without any major problems.

"Yahoo!" Shira called as she got up from the
floor. "That was awesome!"

Chelsea walked over to Jasmine. "Thanks.
That was great."

Jasmine smiled. "We're a team again."

Chelsea nodded. "And we're gonna kick butt
at finals!"

"But first we have to clean our dance," Shira
said. "How're we going to do that without a
teacher?"

The girls fell silent.

"You're not." Miss Carina strode into the
middle of the room.

Ten

Jasmine gulped. Here it came. Miss Carina was going to yell at them again and change the whole thing.

The teacher looked straight at Jasmine. "That was good. Very good."

Jasmine sucked in her breath.

"And I owe you an apology."

Jasmine let her breath out in a gasp. Surely Miss Carina had never uttered those words before in her life.

"Sit down, girls. I'd like to talk to you."

Miss Carina's eyes looked puffy.

"I let the stress of preparing for competition get to me," Miss Carina said. "That doesn't excuse my behavior. I never should have yelled at you like that, Shira."

Shira's eyes were huge. "It's okay."

Miss Carina shook her head. "No, it isn't. Jasmine was right. I should have treated you with respect."

Nobody said anything.

"I was sure you would fall apart without me," she said. "But you proved me wrong. You reminded me of why I teach dance in the first place."

"What?" Jasmine asked.

"You mean *pardon*," Miss Carina said.

Jasmine smiled. Miss Carina might treat them with respect now, but she was still strict. And a lot like her grandmother. "Pardon?"

"I teach dance because I love dance, and because of all the amazing students that walk through this door. You girls have so much talent and so much drive. You work hard every day that you're here."

Jasmine couldn't believe she was hearing this from Miss Carina's mouth. Their teacher had never given any indication in the past that she thought they were amazing. If she'd thought about it, Jasmine would have said that Miss Carina was a dance teacher for the money.

But really, how much money could she make running the studio?

"I watched you run the dance just now. You've shown me exactly what this dance is supposed to be about. Coming together as friends."

The girls looked at each other. Jasmine hadn't thought of it that way. Obviously, none of the other girls had either.

"And you've also reminded me that there are more important things than beating InMotion."

Shira shot her hand up.

"Yes, Shira," Miss Carina said with a smile. "Thank you for raising your hand."

"We're glad to have you back. But there's one thing."

Jasmine's face tensed. Was Shira going to ruin this moment?

Shira broke into a grin. "Beating InMotion might not be the most important thing, but we're still gonna kick their butts!"

Everybody laughed, including Miss Carina. "Then let's get to work. We've got one and a half classes left to get this dance in tip-top shape."

* * *

Jasmine sat in the back of the car, fiddling with the zipper of her hoodie.

"Stop worrying," Will said. He reached over and batted her hand away from the zipper.

"I'm nervous!" Jasmine said. "We've worked so hard. What if we fall apart up there?"

Her grandmother turned around in the front seat. "You not fall apart. You know all steps. Remember what we talk about. Be like your great-grandmother. Have so much fun onstage that you forget everything else."

Jasmine nodded. She'd done it in practice. But could she do it onstage, in front of her friends and family? In front of a bunch of strangers? In front of the judges? What about her duet? What if she got stuck halfway through her back roll like she had in practice?

"Don't worry about the judges," Will said, as if he were reading her mind. "If you get nervous, look at me. I'll make you smile." He stuck out his tongue and squished his nose up with a finger so that Jasmine had a view up his nostrils.

She burst out laughing. "Don't you dare do that while I'm dancing! Laughing onstage will definitely not help!"

"We're here," Jasmine's mom said. She pulled into a parking spot and they all got out.

Jasmine grabbed her garment bag and cosmetic case out of the trunk and they walked into the front foyer of Centennial Theater. Dancers were milling about with their families. Jasmine couldn't see anyone from Moondance. A line had formed at the table where entry tickets were being sold. A fluorescent yellow sign pointed to the dancer change rooms.

Jasmine's mom leaned in to give her a kiss. "You'll be great. Break a leg. And have fun!"

Her grandmother pecked her on the cheek. "Your great-grandmother would be proud of you."

Will pulled the funny face again.

Jasmine smiled and gave him a high five. He caught her hand and held it.

"Don't worry. The team is amazing. *You* are amazing."

Jasmine's cheeks flushed. "Thanks." She tried to pull her hand away, but Will held on. He stepped closer to her, staring into her eyes.

"Don't worry about the judges. Imagine that it's just you and me in the room."

Now Jasmine's whole body was flushed. Will released her hand and stepped away.

"See you later," Jasmine squeaked. She spun around and pushed through the door to the change room. As she followed the yellow signs down a corridor, her mind spun. Did Will *like* her? Did she like him that way? Apparently she did, based on the lightning bugs zinging around in her stomach and the way her hand felt like it was on fire where he'd touched it. She was so lost in thought that she almost bumped into a group of girls huddled together, blocking the way.

"Excuse me," Jasmine said.

One of the girls looked up. Jasmine saw that she was wearing an InMotion hoodie.

"Oh look, it's a Moondancer."

"Yeah," Jasmine said. *Nice comeback.*

"You here to get beaten again?" the girl asked.

All thoughts of Will flew out of Jasmine's head. "Are you?"

The girl wrinkled her nose. "Obviously not. Don't you remember? We won last time."

"That's right," a voice said from behind Jasmine. "And that will be your last time."

Jasmine smiled as she recognized Shira's voice.

"Now let us through!" Shira said, and she stepped in front of Jasmine and pushed her way past the other girls.

"Hey, keep your hands off my costume!" one of the girls said.

"Don't worry—I don't want to touch you," Shira said.

Jasmine hurried by the other girls in Shira's wake.

"I can't believe you said that," she whispered.

"Why? They've been saying awful things to us for years. It's time someone gave them what they deserve." She slowed and turned to look at Jasmine, her hand on the door to the change room. "You ready?"

Jasmine shrugged. "I'm nervous."

"You didn't look it when you were talking to them."

"I felt it."

"Everyone feels nervous. Nerves are good. As long as they don't take over." She pushed open the door, and the noise of more than fifty girls getting ready spilled out into the hallway, along with the fruity smells of hair spray and makeup.

Jasmine took a deep breath to try to steady her nerves and almost choked on the hair-spray fumes. She followed Shira into the room and over to the other Moondancers.

Miss Carina was standing beside a coat rack. "Good morning, girls. Hang your garment bags here." She paused and, as she eyed Jasmine, added, "Please."

Jasmine smiled. "Good morning."

"Once you're all in costume, we'll find a spare room for warm-up."

They pulled on their costumes—black tights, shorts and tunics with rhinestone trim. Miss Carina had decided long ago on a minimalist look for this dance. Looking around, Jasmine silently thanked their teacher for the choice. Some of the teams were wearing the worst costumes she'd ever seen. One group even had shimmery blue knee-length shorts with silver-sequined tube tops. Besides being tacky, they showed little rolls of skin around the armpits and stomach of any girl who wasn't stick thin.

Moondance looked elegant. The girls had done their hair and makeup before arriving, but they spent a few minutes touching up, slicking back errant wisps of hair, reapplying lipstick and checking faces in mirrors.

"Right, girls," Miss Carina called. "Line up so I can have a look at you."

They formed a line and Miss Carina walked up and down, inspecting them. Jasmine figured it wasn't much different from an army inspection.

Miss Carina nodded. "You look beautiful, girls, and sharp. I have a good feeling about today."

Jasmine and Shira turned to look at each other. Their eyebrows shot up. A compliment— that was a first.

"Follow me," Miss Carina said. "There's a room at the end of the hall we can use. We have half an hour before you go onstage."

Jasmine's stomach fluttered as they followed Miss Carina out the door. In just over half an hour, they'd be done. No time left for fine-tuning or practicing. Just a chance to get their bodies warm so they could do their best out there. They'd be competing against teams from all over the province. The competition would be even more difficult than it had been at the preliminaries.

The room at the end of the hall was empty. Jasmine could understand why. There were no windows, and it was dark and stale smelling.

"Nice room," Melanie said.

"It isn't pretty, but we'll have it to ourselves," Miss Carina said. "Spread out and we'll do a quick warm-up."

There wasn't much room to spread out, but they found space where they could.

They began the warm-up sequence without music. Jasmine breathed deeply as they began their pliés, ignoring the musty smell. She would think of this move while she was onstage and try to remember the joy it brought her.

As they were doing their kicks, the door opened.

"Uh-oh," Felicity said.

Miss Brandi poked her head into the room.

Miss Carina's leg thunked to the ground. "This room is occupied," she said in a stiff voice.

"I can see that," Miss Brandi said. "I suppose we can't share it."

"No, we certainly cannot," Miss Carina said.

"Fine. We'll look for you from the stage when we get our trophy."

There was a short silence as the door closed behind her.

"I can't believe she said that!" Chelsea shouted.

"No wonder they're so mean," Melanie said.

Miss Carina clapped her hands. "Girls! Get into your spots—we need to keep going with warm-up." Her face was flushed.

Jasmine raised her hand.

"Yes?" Miss Carina said.

Jasmine took a breath. Miss Carina looked as if she might bite someone's head off at any moment. Jasmine wanted to tell her that even though the last few weeks had been tough, she'd still rather dance with her than with Miss Brandi. She decided to go with a simple "Thanks. For everything."

The other girls nodded in agreement.

Miss Carina smiled. Her shoulders dropped three inches. "You're welcome." Her eyes took in all the girls, then focused on Jasmine. "I'm looking forward to working with *all* of you on the lyrical dance team next year."

Eleven

Jasmine stood in the wings of the stage, waiting for their cue. They were dancing on a proper stage. Things felt more official than they had for the preliminaries. But they also felt scarier. Jasmine's stomach flip-flopped. She tried to calm herself by breathing slowly and going over the moves of the dance in her mind.

"Relax," Shira said. "You're awesome. Dance the way you did in practice."

"Except that instead of a mirror there's an audience full of people and a bunch of judges," Jasmine said.

"Forget about them," Shira said. "Imagine a room full of monkeys."

Jasmine started to giggle and punched Shira in the arm. "Don't make me laugh!"

The stagehand nodded to them and whispered, "You're on."

Chelsea, who stood at the front of the line, turned back to make sure they were all ready, then led them onto the stage.

Jasmine was thankful that the first pose involved kneeling with her head down. She couldn't bear to look at the audience while she waited for the music to start.

The first notes sounded, and Jasmine carefully counted the beats, raising her arms like a butterfly with the rest of the back row. As she stood, she realized she was doing exactly what she'd always done, focusing on the steps and the counts. What had happened to feeling the emotion of the dance?

She had a moment of panic. She was letting the team down. What was she supposed to be feeling right now? Joy at the new day. But Jasmine didn't feel any joy right now.

At that moment, she looked out at the audience and caught sight of Will, her grandmother and her mom. All three of them were sitting on the edges of their seats, huge smiles on their faces.

They didn't care whether her team won. They were here to enjoy watching her dance. That right there was reason for joy. And suddenly, Jasmine didn't need to worry about the steps anymore.

She began listening to the music, not to remember exactly what she should be doing, but to know how she should feel. Her joy turned to sadness during her partner work with Chelsea, then to fear as they moved across the stage and to anger when she encountered the forest creatures.

She felt her joy come back during her duet. Her back roll went off without a hitch. When Shira tapped her on the shoulder, she really felt she was hugging a long-lost friend.

As they formed a line for the triple pirouettes and axels, Jasmine's heart jolted. Would she make it? She couldn't let the team down now. Her eyes sought out Will again. There he was, smiling like a maniac and bending his arms. "Deeper!" he mouthed.

She knew exactly what he meant. Plié. Her smile grew wider. She'd done it before, and she could do it now. With a deep bend in her knees, she pushed off and spun once, twice, three times, finishing with the music, even if a little dizzy.

They leaped and turned their way down the line in their celebration moves. Jasmine soared as she jumped up, threw out her arms and tucked in her legs. Almost before she knew it, they were running back to their circle, holding hands and swaying. Jasmine felt like they should be coming together for a big group hug. This was her team. Will was right—they were amazing.

They joined hands for the layback. Jasmine gave Chelsea an extra squeeze on the arm, and they smiled at each other before leaning backward. Jasmine was vaguely aware of whoops and applause from the audience as she pulled herself up, spun and slid to the floor.

She paused, enjoying the sound of the audience cheering, then pushed herself up and ran to the final pose. They'd done it. She didn't know about anyone else, but that was the best she'd ever danced. She'd hardly been aware of the audience at all, let alone the judges. It was the most fun she'd ever had onstage. She didn't care if they won or not. She wanted to perform all over again.

"Ready, and..." called Chelsea.

They rose and filed offstage to the sound of cheering from the audience.

Miss Carina was waiting for them backstage, tears in her eyes.

"Oh no," Shira said. "Were we that bad?"

Miss Carina shook her head. "You were beautiful. I'm so proud of you."

* * *

Jasmine chewed on a cuticle as they waited for the judges to make their announcement. Her team had joined the audience to watch the last few dances.

There was a lull as the judges left the theater to discuss their notes and choose the winners. The noise level rose as the audience began talking.

"Warning, hot boy approaching on the left," Shira said, nudging Jasmine in the ribs.

Jasmine turned around. "Shira, it's just Will."

"Exactly," Shira said.

Jasmine kicked Shira, trying to ignore the way her heart had started racing. "Hey, Will. What did you think?"

"You guys rocked," he said, perching on the arm of Jasmine's seat.

Shira batted her eyelashes at him. Jasmine wanted to throw up. "What about InMotion?"

Will twisted his lips. "They were pretty good too, like always. But I think you were better."

The emcee walked onstage, and a hush fell over the crowd.

"Guess I'd better get back to my seat," Will said. He leaned over and pecked Jasmine on the cheek. "Good luck."

Jasmine and Shira watched him walk away.

"So gorgeous," Shira said.

"Cut it out."

"Ooh," Shira said. "I think you're jealous."

"Am not."

"That's okay," Shira said. "I'll back off."

"Shira! We're only friends."

"Right." Shira snickered. "That's why you're touching your cheek where he kissed it?"

Jasmine dropped the hand to her lap. She hadn't realized she'd been doing that. Before Jasmine could respond, Robyn leaned over and asked, "Do you think he was right when he said we were better than InMotion?"

"I don't know," Jasmine said. "But you know what? I don't really care."

"Huh?" Robyn said.

"We danced our best, and I don't know about you, but I loved being onstage today. If we win, it will be like a bonus. If we don't win, I still had fun."

Robyn raised her eyebrows as if she didn't really believe Jasmine.

The emcee had finished his preamble. "And now, in third place, InMotion!" There was an intake of breath along the row beside Jasmine as the InMotion girls ran for the stage, a lot more subdued than when they'd placed first in the preliminaries. What did this mean for Moondance? Had they not even placed? They hadn't seen the other teams, so they had no idea.

"In second place, for the very first time, Moondance Studio!"

Jasmine leaped to her feet with her teammates, and they ran for the stage.

"And our winners, Pemberton Dance!"

As a group of girls in blue leotards ran to the stage, Jasmine looked down the line of her teammates. Their faces glowed as they clutched their second-place ribbons. Beyond them, the InMotion girls held their third-place ribbons and stared at the crowd with small smiles.

Sure, it felt good to beat InMotion, but she had spoken the truth earlier. If they hadn't placed, she wouldn't have cared. They'd danced their best and they'd danced as a team. Jasmine had reveled in the joy of dance and the joy of performing. And that was definitely something to celebrate.

Acknowledgments

As I wrote this story, I heard the voices of my dance instructors, past and present, urging me to point my toes, straighten my legs and keep my core muscles engaged. I'm grateful to you all for helping me find the joy in music and movement.

Thanks to Sarah Harvey for her excellent editorial advice and to Stella, Nancy, Libby, Becky, Katherine, Mary and Sue, who helped make my manuscript so much better before it hit Sarah's desk.

Without my cheering squad in Whistler and Vancouver, writing wouldn't be nearly so much fun. Thank you Duane, Ben, Julia, Johanne, Norm, Heather, Doug, Connor, Annie and Lucy for championing my work, reading my drafts, loving me and making me smile.

SARA LEACH lives in Whistler, BC. When she isn't writing, she works as a teacher-librarian, hikes, skis and dances. She especially loves tap and jazz. Her other books with Orca include *Jake Reynolds: Chicken or Eagle?* and the Red Cedar Award-winning *Count Me In*. For more information, visit saraleach.com.